THE ESCAPE

A CLASSIC STORY OF SUSPENSE
ADAPTED BY
J.B. STAMPER

SCHOLASTIC INC.

New York   Toronto   London   Auckland   Sydney
Mexico City   New Delhi   Hong Kong

COVER ILLUSTRATION BY

PATRICK FARICY

INTERIOR ILLUSTRATIONS BY

MIKE BIEGEL

Copyright © 1999 by Scholastic Inc.
All rights reserved. Published by Scholastic Inc.
Printed in the U.S.A.

ISBN 0-439-05703-5

SCHOLASTIC, READ 180, and associated logos and designs are
trademarks and/or registered trademarks of Scholastic Inc.
LEXILE is a trademark of MetaMetrics, Inc.

5   6   7   8   9   10   23   06   05   04   03

TABLE OF CONTENTS

Boris has been given the worst news a prisoner can get. He is going to solitary.

CHAPTER 1

Boris looked down the long, dark hall of the prison. It looked endless.

He was being taken to a place that few people had seen. But everyone feared it. Solitary. The other prisoners said the word with a shudder.

Behind him, the guard laughed. "Well, this will teach you a lesson," he said. "Once you've been in solitary, there will be no more bad behavior from you."

Boris forced his feet down the hall. He knew there was no hope for him.

Seven years ago, he had committed a crime. It was a crime so terrible that even he could not believe that he had done it.

Now he was in prison for the rest of his life.

He was trapped like an animal in a cage. He could not face it any longer!

That's why he had tried to escape.

It had been just after sunset. He was all alone in the yard. The guard who was supposed to be there had made a mistake. He had left Boris alone.

Boris had run for the wall like an animal. He had climbed up and was almost over. Then he had heard the words, "Freeze, prisoner!"

And he had frozen.

That was just yesterday. Now he was headed to an even worse cage.

"You don't have to put me in solitary," Boris said to the guard in a scared voice. "I'll never try that again. I promise!"

The guard just laughed. "You'll learn your lesson," he said again. "Maybe they'll let you out after a few months. But you're a tough one. I know what you did to get inside. You don't deserve anybody's pity."

Boris felt hopeless. It was no good trying.

4

He would just have to deal with it, somehow.

They were coming to the end of the hall. Boris saw the door at the end. He saw the bars across the small window in the door.

He knew that this was it. The others had told him what it would be like inside.

They were right. The guard unlocked three locks. Then he swung open the door. He pushed Boris inside.

The room was like a pen. It was long and narrow, with one bed. High up there was a small window with bars across it.

The walls were of old, rough stone. To Boris, it felt as if they were closing in on him.

His breath started to come in short gasps. His heart pounded. Boris turned to the guard.

"No," he begged. "I can't take it in here. Let me go back to where I was. I'll never do anything wrong again."

"You should have thought of that before," the guard said. Then he slammed the door in Boris's face.

Boris reached for the door. He grabbed the bars in his hands and tried to shake them.

"You'll be sorry!" he yelled after the guard.

The guard just looked back and laughed.

Boris sat down on the bed. He shut his eyes. He didn't want to look around the cell. He was afraid that he would lose his mind.

Thunder woke Boris from a terrible nightmare. In the nightmare, rats were running at him, screeching.

He opened his eyes. He was afraid that the rats were really there. He hated rats more than anything. It was his biggest worry . . . that there might be rats in solitary.

Boris looked around the cell. It was almost dark. Then a flash of lightning lit up the room. Boris jumped in fear.

There was a loud crack of thunder. Then another streak of lightning lit up the cell. The light fell on the wall at the head of his bed.

In those few seconds of light, Boris saw

something that made his heart leap. One of the stones in the wall looked different. There was a thin crack in the cement around it.

Boris tried to fight off a new feeling of hope. But he couldn't stop himself.

Maybe another prisoner had dug around the rock. No one could see the crack unless they were lying on the bed. He had only seen it because of the lightning.

His hands were shaking. He reached down and grabbed the large stone. He moved it back and forth.

Then, suddenly, it came loose! Boris pulled, and the rock fell forward into his hands.

As Boris stared into the hole left by the rock, a flash of lightning lit it up. A tunnel stretched before him . . . with a rat hurrying down into it.

If you were Boris and were afraid of rats, would you enter the tunnel?

Boris has found a tunnel. It is his only chance for freedom. But what about the rats?

CHAPTER 2

Boris jumped back in horror when he saw the rat. He thought about putting the large stone back in place.

Then another flash of lightning cut through the darkness of the cell. The tunnel lit up in front of him. It seemed to welcome him to freedom.

Boris measured the size of the tunnel with his eyes. It was narrow at the beginning. But then it became wider. It looked wide enough for him to crawl through.

Another flash of lightning lit up the tunnel. He searched for any sign of the rat.

"Maybe I didn't see it at all," Boris said to himself. "Maybe it was just a shadow of my nightmare."

Boris looked into the tunnel. He saw no sign of the rat. But his eyes fell on something else. There was a scrap of paper lying on the tunnel floor.

He reached in and pulled it out. He felt its dry surface. The paper was wrinkled with age.

He waited for the lightning to light up the cell again. When it did, he quickly read the message on the paper.

"To the next prisoner who finds this paper," Boris read. "I escaped the horror of this cell by this tunnel. May you share my good luck."

The light faded away before Boris could finish reading the message. He sat in the darkness, shaking with fear and hope.

The message seemed to be written in a dark red liquid. He guessed that it was the blood of the person who had written it.

At last, the lightning came again. He read on, "This is the only way out!" The message was signed with two initials, "T.K."

Just then, Boris heard the guard's footsteps outside his cell. He threw himself over the stone and hole. He pressed his body against the wall.

He waited as the footsteps came to a stop outside his cell.

Then the footsteps moved away. They slowly went down the hallway. Finally, the noise faded into the night.

Suddenly, Boris knew he could not wait any longer. He stuck his head into the tunnel and pushed the rest of his body through.

He tried to look back, but the tunnel was too narrow. There was no turning back now.

Boris squirmed deeper and deeper into the tunnel. Crawling on his stomach, he felt like a snake slithering into its hole. He felt the tunnel grow damper and colder.

Just as the tunnel began to grow slimy, it opened up and became wider.

Boris stood up on his trembling legs. He tried to see into the darkness ahead. He put his hands out in front of him and walked slowly through the black tunnel.

The rocky walls were sharp and tore at his hands. He wiped the sweat from his forehead with one hand and felt warm blood oozing from it.

Boris felt sick. His legs became weak with fear. He dropped to his knees and fell forward onto his hands. Then he felt tiny, clawed feet run over his fingers.

Boris heard his own scream echo and echo through the tunnel.

What should Boris do now? Go on? Or turn back?

Boris finds out that there are rats everywhere!
How could it get any worse?

CHAPTER 3

Once again, the tiny claws of a rat dug into his hands. Boris jumped to his feet, hitting his head on the low ceiling of the tunnel.

Then he felt them all around him. The rats were running over his shoes. They were clawing at his legs.

Boris opened his mouth to scream. But he knew he had to be quiet. He dug a fist into his mouth. He made himself move forward into the tunnel.

He hoped that the rats would not climb up his leg. If they did, he knew he would lose his mind.

Suddenly, the tunnel sloped down at a sharp angle. Boris's feet slipped forward. He landed on his back. He slid deeper and deeper into the tunnel. He no longer felt the rats around him. He no longer heard their claws scratching the rock.

Boris came to a stop where the floor of the tunnel suddenly became flat. His breath was coming in short gasps that tore at his lungs.

He picked himself up. He reached for the slimy walls of the tunnel that he had just fallen down.

Then the truth hit him like a blow. He could never go back. The walls of the tunnel behind him were too steep and slippery.

He had only one chance. He had to push on. He had to push on . . . and hope that there was an end to the tunnel.

Boris moved forward. He clawed at the walls with his hands, trying to hurry.

The tunnel was beginning to feel more and more narrow. His breath was coming in shorter and shorter gasps.

Then the tunnel made a sharp turn to the left. Suddenly Boris saw something that made him cry out with relief. Through an opening in the distance, he could see the pale rays of the moon.

He was almost there. He could smell the night air. Boris struggled toward the patch of moonlight ahead of him.

The tunnel was turning upward. Boris had to grab both sides of the wall and dig his feet into cracks in the wall. Slowly, he pulled himself up.

His hands were becoming more and more torn by the sharp rocks. Boris felt the blood from his cuts run down into his sleeves.

But the pain didn't matter. All that mattered was the patch of light ahead. Boris felt the night air against his face. He was close now. Close to freedom.

Then a sound behind him scared him. It was the sound of those clawed feet. They were following him.

Boris scrambled up to the top of the tunnel even faster. The moonlight was so bright now

that he could see his hands in front of him. He felt a rat brush against his leg. But he had only a few yards to go.

With his last bit of strength, Boris pushed himself toward the light. He felt his head crash into something hard and cold. For a moment he was stunned.

Then he opened his eyes. In front of him, the moon shone through the bars of a heavy gate. Still pressed up against it were the cold, white bones . . . of a skeleton.

There was no escape. There was no going back. This was it. Just Boris . . . and the rats.

Did you think Boris would make it? Are you surprised? Did you want him to escape?

DID YOU LIKE THIS BOOK?

Here are two other READ 180 Paperbacks that you might like to read.

FRANKENSTEIN

The story of the most horrifying— and the most famous—monster of all time.

BY TERRY WEST, BASED ON THE NOVEL BY MARY SHELLEY

CREATURES INFEST LOCAL SCHOOL!

Late at night, strange and mean little creatures are running through the halls of a school. What are they— and what could they possibly want?

BY C.J. HENDERSON

GLOSSARY

behavior	the way someone acts
cell	a room in a prison in which prisoners are locked up
echo	a repeating sound
narrow	not wide
oozed	flowed out slowly
pity	a feeling of sorrow or sympathy for the suffering of another
scrambled	rushed or struggled to get somewhere
shudder	a violent shake from cold or fear
slimy	soft and slippery
slithering	slipping and sliding along, like a snake
sloped	at an angle
solitary	alone; not seeing or talking to anyone
squirmed	moved around uncomfortably
stunned	shocked
trembling	shaking